DOCTOR WHO

The
Time of Angels

Written by Trevor Baxendale

Based on the television scripts 'The Time of Angels'
and 'Flesh and Stone' by Steven Moffat

Published by Pearson Education Limited, Edinburgh Gate, Harlow, Essex, CM20 2JE
Registered company number: 872828

www.pearsonschools.co.uk

Text © Pearson Education 2011

Designed by www.arnosdesign.co.uk

BBC (word mark and logo) is a trade mark of the British Broadcasting Corporation and are used under licence.

The right of Trevor Baxendale to be identified as author of this work has been asserted by him in accordance with the Copyright, Designs and Patents Act 1988.
The Time of Angels is based on the television scripts 'The Time of Angels' and 'Flesh and Stone' by Steven Moffat.

First published 2011

15 14 13 12
10 9 8 7 6 5 4 3

British Library Cataloguing in Publication Data
A catalogue record for this book is available from the British Library

ISBN 978 1 408 27413 2

Printed and bound in Malaysia, (CTP-PPSB)

Acknowledgements
We would like to thank the children and teachers of Bangor Central Integrated Primary School, NI; Bishop Henderson C of E Primary School, Somerset; Brookside Community Primary School, Somerset; Cheddington Combined School, Buckinghamshire; Cofton Primary School, Birmingham; Dair House Independent School, Buckinghamshire; Deal Parochial School, Kent; Newbold Riverside Primary School, Rugby and Windmill Primary School, Oxford for their invaluable help in the development and trialling of the Bug Club resources.

Every effort has been made to contact copyright holders of material reproduced in this book. Any omissions will be rectified in subsequent printings if notice is given to the publishers.

Contents

Prologue   4

Chapter 1   7

Chapter 2   11

Chapter 3   14

Chapter 4   20

Chapter 5   23

Chapter 6   29

Chapter 7   34

Chapter 8   38

Chapter 9   42

Chapter 10   49

Chapter 11   55

Chapter 12   59

Chapter 13   63

PROLOGUE

Inside the TARDIS, the Doctor's time machine, the Doctor was working frantically at the controls. His mop of brown hair bounced over his eyes. He looked like a young man but he was more than 900 years old.

"What's happening?" asked his companion, Amy Pond.

"Someone on a spaceship in the 51st century is trying to attract my attention," he explained.

The scanner screen flickered into life. It showed the blackness of deep space, a thousand stars and a spaceship. It was as sleek and silver as a bullet.

Amy watched as a tiny porthole opened on the side of the spaceship. A figure emerged and shot out into space. Amy blinked. Nothing could survive long out in space, alone.

The Doctor sprinted down the steps to the TARDIS doors and flung them open. He was just in time – a woman shot through and landed on top of the Doctor.

"Hello, sweetie," she said.

"River Song!" cried the Doctor in surprise. He sounded delighted and worried at the same time.

River Song picked herself up and looked out through the open doors. The silver spaceship was shrinking into the distance.

"Follow that spaceship!" she ordered.

CHAPTER 1

River Song was an old friend of the Doctor. Amy couldn't help but like her – she was warm and jolly and seemed to know just how to handle the Doctor.

River was standing by the Doctor who was struggling to keep the TARDIS on course.

"They've gone into warp drive," he said. "We're losing them!"

River took over the TARDIS controls, much to Amy's amazement. "How does she know how to fly the TARDIS?" Amy whispered to the Doctor.

"Call that flying the TARDIS?" snorted the Doctor. "Ha!"

River looked up and smiled. "Got them," she said. "We've caught up and landed."

"What?" The Doctor frowned. "We can't have landed. It didn't make the noise."

"What noise?"

The Doctor imitated the strange wheezing noise the TARDIS always made when it landed.

"It's not supposed to make that noise," River told him. "You just leave the brakes on."

The Doctor sulked. "Well, it's a brilliant noise."

Unlike the TARDIS, the spaceship hadn't landed. It had crashed – nose-first into what looked like the ruins of an ancient castle built on cliffs overlooking the sea.

The TARDIS had landed on the beach, surrounded by pieces of the shattered spaceship. On one of the pieces was the spaceship's name: *Byzantium*.

"What caused it to crash?" wondered River Song, looking up at the wreckage.

"I'm not sure," admitted the Doctor. "According to the TARDIS, the engines were going into phase-shift as it approached the planet. There were no survivors."

"At least the building was empty," said River. "It's an old Aplan temple. It's been unoccupied for centuries. There is *one* survivor though."

The Doctor frowned, puzzled.

"There's a thing in the belly of that ship that can never die," said River.

A look of deep concern settled on the Doctor's face and Amy felt a chill run through her.

River Song took out a communicator and spoke into it. "You lot in orbit yet?" she asked. "I'm at the crash site. Teleport down to my signal."

Seconds later, four soldiers materialised nearby. The leader was a tall, craggy-looking man. He stalked across the sand towards River.

River introduced the soldier to her friend. "This is the Doctor."

The soldier looked at the Doctor, impressed. It was almost as if, thought Amy, the Doctor had some kind of reputation.

"Father Octavian, sir," the soldier introduced himself. "Bishop, second class. I have twenty clerics at my command. The rest of my men are in a troopship ready to come down. Dr Song was helping us with our investigation. Has she explained to you what we're dealing with?"

The Doctor narrowed his eyes, intrigued.

River Song stepped forward. "Doctor, what do you know of the Weeping Angels?"

CHAPTER 2

Night fell quickly on the planet. Father Octavian's troops teleported down and set up a base by the cliffs beneath the Aplan temple.

At a command station, Octavian briefed the Doctor and Amy.

"The Angel is still trapped in the crashed spaceship," he said. "Our mission is to get inside and destroy it."

They looked up at the wreck of the *Byzantium*.

"We can't get in from the top," explained Octavian. "But according to our scans, there is a network of catacombs leading right up to the temple. We can blow a hole in the base of the cliff, then work our way up."

As Octavian moved away to organise things, Amy tapped the Doctor on the shoulder. "So, this Weeping Angel thing. It's pretty bad, yeah?"

The Doctor looked deeply unhappy. "A Weeping Angel is the deadliest, most powerful life form evolution has ever produced. Right now, one of them is trapped inside that wreckage."

He was about to say more but River Song, now dressed in her combat gear, called from one of the military command huts. "Doctor! Father Octavian! Come and look."

Inside the metal hut, there was a fuzzy image on a TV monitor. "It's from the security cameras in the *Byzantium* vault," River explained. "It's only four seconds long."

On the screen was the flickering image of a stone statue, covering its face with its hands.

"It's just a statue," said Amy.

"It's a statue when you see it," nodded River.

"What do you mean, it's a statue when you see it?" asked Amy, peering at the screen.

"The Weeping Angels can only move if they're unseen," replied River. "So legend has it."

"It's not legend," said the Doctor. "It's a quantum lock. In the sight of any living creature, the Angels cease to exist. They're just stone. The ultimate defence mechanism."

"Being stone?" smiled Amy.

"Being stone ... until you turn your back."

CHAPTER 3

"We have to proceed with caution.
The hyperdrive would have split
open on impact," the Doctor explained
to Octavian later, when they were planning
what to do. "The whole ship will be flooded with
radiation – deadly to almost any living thing."

"Deadly to an Angel?" asked Octavian.

"Dinner to an Angel," replied the Doctor. "The
longer we leave it in there, the more it will feast on the
radiation and the stronger it will grow."

Octavian signalled to his men. "Prepare the
explosives."

River called to the Doctor. "Look, I found this book.
It's all about the Weeping Angels. I've marked a few
passages that might be of interest."

The Doctor took the book and began to flick through it. His mind soaked up the information in seconds.

Meanwhile, Amy was alone in the metal hut. She was curious about this Weeping Angel so she stepped towards the monitor to take a closer look. That was strange – the statue seemed to have moved. Its face was no longer hidden by its hands.

"Dr Song!" Amy called from the entrance of the hut. "Did you have more than one clip of the Angel?"

"No, just the four seconds," replied Dr Song.

Amy frowned and went back to the monitor. It still only showed the four seconds River Song had recorded. Yet the Weeping Angel had definitely moved. It was now facing the screen, with its hands by its sides. It was just like the Doctor and River had said: the statue only moved when you weren't looking at it ...

Amy was so intent on the image of the Angel that she idn't notice the door of the hut locking behind her.

Outside, the Doctor was still flicking through the Weeping Angels book.

"Something's wrong with this book, " he grumbled. Then he realised what was missing. "Pictures! Why aren't there any pictures?"

The Doctor held up the book to River Song. "This whole book is a warning about the Weeping Angels," he said. "So why are there no pictures?"

"There was a bit about images somewhere," River said.

"Oh, hang on ..." The Doctor flicked through the book again. "Here it is: *'That which holds the image of an angel becomes itself an angel'*."

"Now, what exactly does that mean?" wondered the Doctor.

Inside the hut, Amy kept her eyes fixed on the image of the Angel. That way she knew it couldn't move again. Amy's hands searched for the remote control. She found it and pressed the off button.

The TV flickered, went blank, then immediately came back on.

Amy switched it off again – but the image was still there. It was as if the Weeping Angel had taken control of the screen.

"You're just a recording," Amy said uneasily. "You can't move."

She tried to unplug the monitor, but it was jammed in place. When she looked back up, the Angel's face filled the screen. The statue was staring right into her eyes.

She ran to the door of the hut, but discovered it was locked.

Amy glanced back at the screen.

To her horror, the Angel's face had changed again. It was no longer serene and blank. Its mouth was wide open revealing sharp, threatening fangs.

Amy desperately tried to open the door. She called out to the Doctor, but the walls of the hut were reinforced armour plate. No one could hear unless they were right next to the hut.

She looked back at the monitor screen and gasped. In front of the screen, suspended in mid-air, was a full-sized image of the Angel.

"Doctor!" Amy screamed. "It's in the room!"

Doctor slammed the book shut. "Amy!" He suddenly
embered he had left her alone, with a recording of a
ping Angel.

*hat which holds the image of an angel becomes
'f an angel.*

he Doctor dashed back to the hut and banged on the
. "Amy! What's happening?"

Doctor! The Angel's coming out of the screen!"

Can you turn the screen off?" shouted the Doctor.

've tried."

Try again, but don't take your eyes off the Angel! It
t move if you're looking. Don't even blink, Amy!"

my stumbled towards the remote control, all the
e keeping her eyes glued to the Angel. They were
ing to water, but she refused to blink.

The flickering image of the Angel stared back at her.

The Doctor's voice came through the door: "Amy, don't look at the eyes. Look at the Angel, but don't look at the eyes!"

Outside, the Doctor was reading from the book again. " *'The eyes are not the windows of the soul, they are the doors. Beware what may enter there.'*"

The image of the Angel flickered again. Suddenly, Amy realised something. She held the remote control

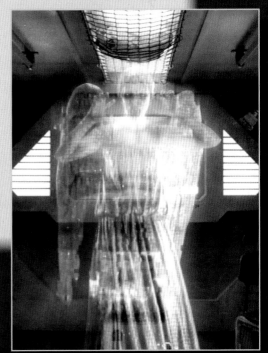

and noticed that every time the loop went back to the start of the four-second recording, the image flickered.

Timing it just right, Amy hit the pause control. The image froze – right in the middle of the flicker.

The Angel was gone. Instead, there was nothing but a
zy grey flicker.

Free of the Angel's power, the door to the hut
ocked. The Doctor and River burst in.

'I froze it!" said Amy. "There was a blip on the tape
I froze it on the blip. It stopped being an Angel."

It got a good look at us though," realised the Doctor.
no longer dormant."

CHAPTER 5

The mission to find and destroy the Angel had started. Octavian's men blew a hole in the cliffs using explosives. Entering through the hole, they reached the caves beneath the temple quite easily.

Their torch beams roved across the rocks, throwing up strange and sinister shadows.

"What is this place?" asked Amy.

"It's an Aplan graveyard," said River Song. Carved into the craggy walls stone walls of the cavern were hundreds of statues.

"I guess this makes our job trickier," said Octavian. "A stone Angel on the loose amongst stone statues."

They moved on, climbing cautiously through the tunnels. The Doctor was exploring the next cavern when he heard gunfire.

He ran back to find a young soldier aiming his weapon. There was gun smoke in the air.

The soldier had been spooked by an old, broken statue.

"What's your name?" the Doctor asked the soldier.

The soldier looked nervous. "Bob, sir."

"It's good that you're scared, Bob, because scared keeps you fast – and fast keeps you safe."

"Right," said Octavian. "We're carrying on." He turned back to Bob. "You stay here and guard the approach."

They moved deeper into the caves, checking every shadow and statue by torchlight.

The Doctor turned to River. "Who did you say built this temple?"

"The Aplans built it. They died out 400 years ago."

The Doctor's torchlight roved around the decayed statues. Most were barely recognisable, the features worn away over time. "I thought the Aplans had two heads."

"They did," replied River.

"Then why haven't the statues?"

Everyone checked the nearest statue. Each had only one head.

"Octavian, I apologise," said the Doctor. "I've led you all into terrible danger."

"What do you mean?" asked Octavian.

The Doctor herded everyone into the centre of the cave. "Switch off your torches." They did so, plunging the cave into darkness except for the single beam of light from the Doctor's own torch. He aimed the beam at a group of statues which were facing away from them. "I'm going to switch off my torch as well," he said quietly. "Just for a second."

"Are you sure that's wise?" asked River uneasily.

"No." The Doctor switched his torch off and then on again quickly. The group of statues was now facing him! In that instant of darkness, they had moved.

"These aren't statues of dead Aplans," said the Doctor. "They're Weeping Angels. Every single one of them!"

They all switched their torches back on and looked around the cave at the rows of statues on different levels.

"They've moved!" shouted Amy.

"They're coming after us," realised the Doctor.

"But these don't look like Angels," objected Octavian.

"That's because they're dying," explained the Doctor. "Losing their form. They've been here for centuries, starving."

"Losing their image?" River said.

"Their image is their power." Something occurred to the Doctor as he spoke. "Power! Of course! All that radiation leaking out of the spaceship. The crash of the *Byzantium* wasn't an accident – it was a rescue mission for the Angels. We're in the middle of an army and it's waking up!"

Octavian unhooked his radio and called the cleric on sentry duty at the entrance. "Bob – come in please. Are you there, Bob?"

A voice crackled over the radio: *"Bob here, sir."*

"All the statues are active," warned Octavian.

"I know, sir. They killed the other guards, sir."

The Doctor took the radio from Octavian. "Bob, it's me, the Doctor. Where are you now?"

"I'm on my way up to you, sir."

"That's good, Bob. Tell me – how did you escape?"

"I didn't escape, sir. The Angel killed me, too."

"If you're dead, how can I be talking to you?"

"You're not talking to me, sir. The Angel has no voice
) it's using me to talk to you."

"So when you say you're on your way up, what you
ally mean is ..."

"I'm the Angel. I'm coming up, sir, yes."

The Doctor turned to Octavian. "There's no way
k."

)ctavian nodded. "Then we keep going forwards!"

CHAPTER 6

Eventually they reached the *Byzantium* at the top of the temple. The silver nose of the spaceship had burst through the temple roof. Looking directly up, they could see an entry hatch – but it was twenty metres above them. There was no way to reach it.

"Angels approaching from all sides, sir," reported a cleric.

"The gravity globe is flickering," noted River.

Floating next to the spaceship was a gravity globe – a sphere the size of a football that provided extra light. It contained anti-gravity energy to keep it suspended in the air. The light from the globe was growing dimmer by the second.

"The Angels are draining the power for themselves," said the Doctor. "We *have* to get to that ship."

Octavian's radio buzzed and the Doctor took the call. He knew who it would be.

"Excuse me, sir," said the voice of Bob. *"Your power will not last much longer and the Angels will be with you shortly."*

"Why are you telling me this?"

"There's something the Angels are very keen for you to know, sir."

"Which is?"

"You told me my fear would keep me alive, but it didn't. You let me down. You're trapped, sir, and about to die."

The Doctor's fingers tightened on the radio. He was angry now. "In that case, the Angels have just made a great, big, whopping mistake," he said grimly.

"What mistake, sir?"

"There's one thing you should never, ever put in a trap if you're smart," said the Doctor. "Me!"

He aimed his sonic screwdriver directly upwards, right at the floating gravity globe. Triggering the sonic screwdriver, he caused the globe to overload and the anti-gravity energy burst out in a huge flash.

"Jump, everyone!" shouted the Doctor.

The anti-gravity energy affected everyone jumping up from the cave floor. The Doctor, Amy, River Song, Father Octavian and his clerics began to float up into the air like astronauts in zero gravity.

They flew straight up until they reached the hull of the *Byzantium*.

Then a curious thing happened. The spaceship had its own artificial gravity, which meant that when they reached the hull, they found themselves stuck to it – just as if it were the floor.

"Come on!" cried the Doctor. "Stand up!"

They all got to their feet. They were standing on the *Byzantium* – suspended high over the cavern below. It was as if everything had been turned upside down.

There were Angels in the cavern, looking up at them.

"They're drawing power from the ship," said the Doctor. "Soon they'll be an army. There's no time to lose."

He crouched down by the spaceship's hatch and used his sonic screwdriver to open it. He climbed inside and the others quickly followed.

The hatch sealed shut behind them. Inside was a metal corridor.

"This corridor runs the length of the ship," explained the Doctor.

"Will the Angels follow us?" asked Octavian.

There was a distinct clang from outside the hatch.

"They're already here."

"So we're effectively walking up the inside of a tube," said Amy. "What if the power – and the gravity – fail?"

"We'll all plunge to our deaths," replied the Doctor, comfortingly.

The lights flickered and faded. When they came back on, the hatch was open and there was a Weeping Angel peering through.

CHAPTER 7

"Keep watching them!" ordered Octavian. "They can't move if we can see them!"

"We need to get through the next hatch," said River Song.

The Doctor nodded, working on a control panel. "There – the Angels can't drain the power now."

"Good work, Doctor," Octavian said.

"Except that there's only one way to open this next door," said the Doctor, tapping the interior hatch. "I'll have to divert power from the lights. We'll be in complete darkness, just for a second."

They all looked at the statues. As soon as the lights went out, the Angels would be free to move.

"There's no other way," the Doctor said. He turned to Amy. "When the lights go down, spin this wheel clockwise, four turns."

"Ten."

"No, four. Just four."

"Yes, I heard you."

"Ready!" cried the Doctor – and switched off the lights.

Octavian and his men opened fire at the Angels. As their rifles flashed and roared, the Angels could be seen advancing up the corridor, fangs bared and hands clawed.

Amy heaved at the door wheel. It was very stiff. Eventually the hatch opened, and they all filed quickly through.

It clanged shut behind them.

They were in some kind of control room. The lights were on and the control panels all hummed with power.

"How long have we got?" asked Octavian.

"Five minutes, max," answered the Doctor.

"Nine," said Amy.

"Five," repeated the Doctor. "It won't take the Angels long to break the hatch locks."

"So where do we go now?"

The Doctor ran his hands along the rear wall of the cockpit. At the base was a series of latches, which he unlocked using the sonic screwdriver. Slowly, the entire wall began to slide up into the ceiling to reveal an incredible sight.

Amy stared, open-mouthed.

Beyond the control room, as far as the eyes could see, there were trees and plants emerging from a fine mist.

ıy gasped. "It's a *forest!*"

The Doctor nodded. "Yeah, it's a forest. Also, if we're
ky, an escape route."

"Eight," said Amy. She didn't know why she said that.
e was still staring in amazement at the forest. "Trees
a spaceship!"

"Trees sucking in starlight from deep space and
athing out air for the crew," the Doctor explained. He
pped through the hatch into the forest. "This vault
ıs right through the heart of the ship."

"Seven," said Amy.

"Sorry, what?"

"Nothing."

The Doctor returned to the control room. "You said seven."

"No, I didn't," protested Amy.

"You did," said River.

"Doctor," interrupted Father Octavian. "I've scanned the ship. There's an exit, far end of the forest, into the Primary Flight Deck."

"Good, that's where we need to go."

"Excuse me." Bob's voice came over the intercom. *"Angel Bob here, sir."*

The Doctor dropped into a flight chair. "Ah, Angel Bob. There you are."

"The Angels are wondering what you hope to achieve."

"Achieve? Nothing. It's nice in here – consoles, comfy chairs, a forest. How's things with you?"

"The Angels are feasting, sir. Soon we'll be able to absorb enough power to consume this ship, this world, and all the stars and worlds beyond."

The Doctor shifted in his seat. "Yeah, well, we've got comfy chairs – did I mention them?"

"We have no need of comfy chairs."

The Doctor smiled at Amy. "I made him say 'comfy chairs'!"

"Six," said Amy.

"OK, Bob, enough chat," said the Doctor into the radio. He suddenly sounded very serious. "What I want to know is – what have you done to Amy?"

"There's something in her eye."

"What's in her eye?"

"We are."

"What's he talking about?" asked Amy. "I'm five. I mean, fine."

"You're counting down," said the Doctor. "From ten. You have been for a couple of minutes now. Why?"

Amy frowned. She felt frightened. "Counting down to what?"

"I don't know."

"We shall take her," said Angel Bob's voice. *"We shall take all of you."*

There's nowhere near enough power on this ship for you to do that," argued the Doctor.

"There is more power on this ship than you realise," said Angel Bob.

Then the Doctor saw something that made the hairs on the back of his neck stand up. His blood ran cold.

On the far wall there was a crack. It was in the shape of a crooked smile. It was horribly familiar.

"Doctor," said Amy. She had seen it too. "That's like the crack from my bedroom wall ..."

CHAPTER 9

Amy looked at the crack. What was it doing here, of all places?

Octavian was losing patience. "Doctor, the Angels are almost through. We have to move out!"

With a last anxious look at the crack, the Doctor and Amy followed the troops out of the control room and into the forest.

It wasn't long before River realised that something was wrong. They were moving quickly through the trees, but Amy was hesitating.

"Amy, what's wrong?"

"Four," said Amy. She was still doing it – still counting down from ten to zero, and she had no idea why.

Pale and frightened, she lay down on a tree stump. She felt so weak.

"What's wrong with me?" Amy asked.

"Nothing, you're fine," said River gently.

"Everything, you're dying," said the Doctor. He started to pace around the forest clearing where they had stopped. "Let me think! The Angel said you had something in your eye. Now what could that be?"

Octavian's men positioned themselves around the clearing. One of them spotted an Angel in the woods. Then there was another, and another, all peering at them from the surrounding trees.

"Keep your eyes on them," warned Octavian. "Do not let them move!"

The Doctor was still thinking furiously. "You stared at the image of the Angel on the screen ..."

"The image of an Angel is an Angel," said Amy weakly.

"Yes, and we stare at them so they can't move," the Doctor realised. "We don't even blink and that's *exactly* what they want. As long as our eyes are open, they can climb inside. There's an Angel in your mind!"

"Three," said Amy. "Doctor, I'm scared. I can feel it coming ..."

"Counting down – what's that about?" the Doctor wondered. He grabbed the radio. "Angel Bob, why are they making her count?"

"To make her afraid, sir."

"OK, but why? What for?"

"For fun, sir."

The Doctor threw the radio down in frustration. "So there's an Angel in Amy's mind, like a virtual image. It's coming to kill her. So how do we stop it? How do we stop that image? How do we stop seeing something?" A thought struck him and he whirled to face Amy. "Close your eyes! Amy, close your eyes now!"

"I don't want to."

"Good, that's the Angel speaking. It doesn't want you to close your eyes. So close them, Amy!"

At the Doctor's order, Amy shut her eyes tight.

River ran a medical scanner over Amy. "She's stabilised," she said with a sigh of relief.

"Can I open my eyes now?" Amy asked.

The Doctor sat down next to her. "Amy, listen to me. If you open your eyes now for more than a second, you will die. The Angel is still inside you. We haven't stopped it – just paused it. You've almost used up your countdown so you mustn't open your eyes."

"Doctor," said Octavian. "We have to move out. We're too exposed here."

There was nothing else for it. The Doctor and River would have to carry on with Octavian, heading for the Primary Flight Deck of the crashed spaceship. Amy couldn't travel with her eyes shut, so she would stay put with some of Octavian's men to guard her.

"You'll be safer here," the Doctor told Amy. "We can't protect you on the move. I'll be back for you as soon as I can. Just keep those eyes closed!"

He stood up and called out to the soldiers at the edge of the clearing. "Keep watching the forest and stop those Angels getting any closer. We'll be back soon!"

With one last glance at Amy, still sitting alone on the tree stump with her eyes tightly closed, the Doctor turned and ran after River and Octavian.

"What's so dangerous about a crack in the wall?" asked River Song as they rushed through the trees.

"My theory?" replied the Doctor. "The end of the universe – a big bang, so big that it caused every moment in history, past and future, to crack."

"Well, whatever it is, we'd better hurry," River said. "Time's running out."

The Doctor looked sharply at her. "What did you say?"

"Time's running out."

"Yes ..." The Doctor looked thoughtful. "What if time could really run out?"

CHAPTER 10

In the forest clearing, Octavian's men were getting jumpy. The Angels were creeping closer and closer.

"What's happening?" Amy demanded. "Tell me – I can't see!"

Suddenly, a brilliant glare lit up part of the forest.

"What's that?" asked one soldier, shielding his eyes.

All around the clearing, the Weeping Angels moved back from the brightly shining light.

"It's like they're running away," said the soldier, "as if they're scared of it."

By now Amy was getting very worried. She only had less than two seconds of her countdown left. If she opened her eyes for just a moment, she could at least glimpse what had caused the Angels to run. She could shut them again almost instantly.

Amy had never turned away from a challenge in her life. She decided to risk it. She had to know what was going on.

She opened her eyes.

The bright light was seeping through the forest. Beyond the trees Amy could see where it was coming from – a jagged gash in the air, in the shape of a crooked smile.

"It's the crack in my wall," she whispered in disbelief, then snapped her eyes shut.

The Doctor, River and Octavian had reached the Primary Flight Deck. River went in first but, as Octavian went to follow, a Weeping Angel suddenly appeared behind him. It slid its arm around his neck.

The Doctor looked back and the Angel froze into a statue.

"Let him go," said the Doctor.

"It can't let me go," said Octavian, struggling to speak. "Not while you're looking at it."

"I can't stop looking at it," the Doctor protested. "It'll kill you."

"It's going to kill me anyway. There's no way out of this. You have to leave me."

"Can't you wriggle out?"

"No. It's too tight. You have to leave me, sir. There's nothing you can do." The statue's arm was like a stone vice around his throat.

"But you're dead if I leave you," said the Doctor.

Octavian gritted his teeth. "Sir, the Angels are coming. You have to leave me!"

"You'll die."

"Then I will die in the knowledge that my courage did not desert me at the end."

The Doctor nodded sadly. "I wish I'd known you better."

"I think, sir, you know me at my best."

There was no other choice. The Doctor knew that if he were to save Amy and River, and perhaps stop the Angels once and for all, he had to get inside the Primary Flight Deck. That meant leaving Octavian to his fate.

With a final sad smile of farewell, the Doctor turned and sprinted for the hatch. He hurled himself through it, knowing that Octavian would now be dead.

Meanwhile, back in the clearing, two of the soldiers had been sent to investigate the crack.

They had disappeared. More worryingly, the other soldier who had stayed with Amy seemed to have forgotten his fellow soldiers.

"How could you forget them?" Amy asked. "They were here just a minute ago. You sent them to look!"

"Sent who?" asked the soldier blankly. He couldn't even remember who they were. It was as if, having walked into the light of the time crack, all memory of the soldiers had vanished.

"Listen," said the remaining soldier. "I need to get a closer look at that light, whatever it is. I'll be back in a minute."

"No!" protested Amy. "Don't go! You won't come back – just like the others."

"What others?"

"Don't go. You mustn't."

"Here." The soldier pressed a radio into Amy's hand. "Spare communicator. I'll stay in touch the whole time."

It was no use Amy protesting. The soldier moved away towards the light.

CHAPTER 1

Amy spoke into the radio. "Hello? Can you hear me?"

The soldier's voice came back quite clearly: "It's me. I'm near the crack now."

"Come back, please," pleaded Amy.

"It's weird looking at it," said the soldier's voice. "It feels really –"

"Really what? Hello?"

There was no answer. The soldier had gone – just like the others.

Then another voice crackled through the radio. It was a wonderfully familiar one. "Amy? Hello? Is that you?"

"Doctor!" Amy cried with relief.

"We've reached the Primary Flight Deck," said the Doctor. "Octavian didn't make it, but there's a teleport system here and River is trying to get it working. Where are you? Are the soldiers still with you?"

"They've gone. There was a light and they walked into it. They didn't even remember each other."

"They wouldn't remember, Amy," the Doctor explained, "because the moment they went into that light, they were erased from history."

"What is that light?" wondered River from the Flight Deck.

"Time running out," said the Doctor. "The closer someone gets to the light, the more of their life gets erased. That's why the Angels are trying to move away from it."

"What am I going to do?" asked Amy.

"Come to us on the Primary Flight Deck."

Amy clutched her radio tightly. "I can't open my eyes – I can't even see! What about the Weeping Angels?"

"All the Angels will do is kill you," replied the Doctor.

That sounded bad enough to Amy. "What?"

"There is energy running out of that crack which, if it touches you, will erase you from history." The Doctor sounded desperate. "You will never have lived at all."

River looked up from the controls on the Flight Deck. "What's that noise?" There was a bumping and scraping outside the walls.

"It's the Angels," replied the Doctor. "Running from the time energy. They're right outside."

The noise grew louder. It was the sound of stone on metal. The Angels were trying to get in.

River finished her work on the teleport controls. She threw a lever and suddenly Amy was standing there with her eyes still shut, clutching her radio.

"What happened? Where am I?"

"Safe!" River hugged her. "I teleported you here – homed in on your radio signal."

An alarm sounded and the lights began to dim. "The Angels are draining the last of the ship's power," said the Doctor. "Which means the shield door is going to release ..."

They turned as the huge door to the Flight Deck opened. Outside were hundreds of Weeping Angels.

CHAPTER 12

One of the Angels had a radio communicator in its hand.

"Angel Bob, I presume," said the Doctor.

"The time energy is coming," said Angel Bob's voice over the radio. *"If you throw yourself into the crack, it will close and the Angels will be saved."*

The Doctor considered. It was possible, after all. His sacrifice would be enough to feed the crack, to make it close. "What's in it for me?"

"Your friends will be saved."

River grabbed the Doctor's arm. "Doctor, no! You can't do it!"

"I'm a Time Lord," the Doctor argued. "It could work."

"I've travelled in time, too," said River. "Throw me in!"

"Don't be daft. It doesn't work like that. Get a grip."

River wouldn't listen. "Doctor, I can't let you do this ..."

"No, seriously, get a grip," insisted the Doctor.

"You're not going to die here!"

"No, really! River, Amy, *get a grip!*"

Then River realised what the Doctor was planning to do. "Oh, you genius!" She turned to Amy. "Grab on to something. Hold tight!"

"Sir," said Bob. *"The Angels need you to sacrifice yourself now."*

"The thing is, Bob," replied the Doctor with a smile, "the Angels are draining all the power from this ship, and you know what? They've forgotten where they're standing. They've forgotten the gravity of the situation."

River placed Amy's hands on the edge of a control console. A sign was flashing: GRAVITY FAILING.

"Amy, hold on tight and don't let go for anything."

Then River grabbed a handhold, just as the Doctor turned away from the Angels and grasped the edge of another control panel. As he did so, the *Byzantium's* artificial gravity failed.

The force that had held them all to the deck vanished and was replaced by the planet's own natural gravity – and that was at the bottom of the ship.

The Doctor, Amy and River felt as if everything were tipped sideways. Holding tight onto the control console, they hung with their feet dangling over the hatchway leading to the forest.

The Weeping Angels, frozen as statues, fell backwards, down through the forest, heading for the bright light of the crack.

There was no escape. Every single Angel was engulfed by the fierce glare. Then, with a final blaze of satisfaction, the crack closed and vanished.

CHAPTER 13

Amy was with the Doctor on the beach next to the TARDIS, recovering after the long climb out of the wreckage. She had her eyes open now. It was safe.

"What happened?" asked Amy.

"The Angels all fell into the crack," the Doctor explained. "They were wiped from history and so the Angel in your mind was erased from time too."

The Doctor and Amy said goodbye to River Song, who was being teleported up to a ship in orbit. She had her own life to lead but she told the Doctor that it wouldn't be long before they met again.

"I'll look forward to it," he promised.

They watched her fade away, and then headed for the TARDIS. Moments later the old blue police box faded away too ...